Green Street Mystery

TRACKS IN the NORTH WOODS

By Dana Brenford

CREATED AND EDITED BY

Marion Dane Bauer

ILLUSTRATED BY

Kristi Schaeppi

PUBLISHED BY

CRESTWOOD HOUSE

Mankato, MN, U.S.A.

CIP

LIBRARY OF CONGRESS CATALOGING IN PUBLICATION DATA

Brenford, Dana.
  Tracks in the North Woods

  (A green street mystery series)
  SUMMARY: When twelve-year-old twins Peter and Jason and their stepsister Kim visit Canada's North Woods in the middle of winter, they investigate the disappearance of an elderly woman hermit.
  [1. Mystery and detective stories.   2. Hermits—Fiction.   3. Brothers and sisters—Fiction.]
I. Title. II. Series: Brenford, Dana. Green Street mystery.
PZ7.B7514Tr   1988   [Fic]—dc19   88-21963
ISBN 0-89686-420-0

International Standard Book Number:	Library of Congress Catalog Card Number:
0-89686-420-0	88-21963

Produced by Carnival Enterprises.

Box 3427, Mankato, MN, U.S.A. 56002

CONTENTS

1
MUSH!

The race was set to start before dawn. Dozens of barking sled dogs strained at their harnesses, more than ready to begin. But Peter Riley and his twin brother Jason had to withdraw from their position near the starting line for the third time. They warmed up by a campfire, watching the race preparations through the foggy plumes of their breath. What was the delay now, Peter wondered. He had never been so cold.

"This is really it, guys," their stepsister, Kim Grant, said as she joined them. "It's final. This is what I was meant to do with my life." The pink in Kim's freckled face deepened. "I'm going to be a musher just like Wendy over there. Look at her dogs—they can't wait to hit the trail. It's woman and beast out there together against the elements."

Peter and Jason exchanged here-we-go-again glances. "Let's see," Jason said, scratching the side of his head. "Musher. You're going to drive sled dogs. Is that before or after your career as a test pilot?"

Peter nudged his brother, but Jason continued, "And what about your promising future as an opera singing ballerina?"

"Jason, let her be," Peter said.

But Kim was smiling tolerantly at them both. 'I'll have fifteen huskies mixed with a little hound, like Wendy has. They're great for these long races. They can go hundreds of miles, no sweat."

"Dogs don't sweat," Jason reminded her.

"It's just an expression," Kim said calmly. "Smart aleck."

Peter watched the two of them go at it, something he had been doing a lot since last summer. That was when Jason's and his mother married Kim's father. It wasn't bad having a sister, twelve years old as they were. They even called themselves the Green Street gang. But Peter often found himself acting as referee between Jason and Kim.

The shout of a race official startled him. The first sled-dog team was finally ready. The harnesses were free of tangles and the frantic dogs were held somewhat steady by the musher's support team.

"I know they're to protect the dogs' feet," Kim

said, "but aren't those little booties adorable?"

"Don't use 'adorable' in the paper," Jason told her. He was referring to their newspaper, *The Green Street Reporter.*

Peter agreed. "We've come to the Canadian North Woods to cover a sled-dog marathon, not a doggy fashion show." Actually it was his mother and stepfather who were getting paid to cover this event, but the gang always tagged along and managed to dig out their own stories.

And Peter had an idea he was already onto one. He noticed people scanning the crowd and then joining in tense discussions with their neighbors. He intended to find out what—or whom—they were looking for with such concern.

But just now the race was starting, finally, and everyone's attention was on that alone.

Reluctantly, Peter left the warm fire and followed Kim and Jason back to the starting line. They leaned forward with the crowd for a better view just as the shout, "Mush!" pierced the icy air.

The first driver's dogs were finally silenced as they lunged gratefully ahead. It was still quite dark, and the dogs' eyes, reflecting fire and lamplight, glowed and bobbed toward the cheering crowd. Then the team rushed past in a furry blur and was gone.

Peter memorized the eerie beauty of it for his

article. He couldn't help but wish he were back at home writing up this story instead of enduring the forty-degree-below-zero windchill to get it.

He searched the crowd anxiously for their parents. Shouldn't they all be together, keeping each other warm? Mom was still interviewing, and Dad was still snapping photos of various race participants and officials. Peter knew he should be doing those things too if he ever hoped to be a real reporter someday.

Three other teams had disappeared into the dark now, on the first leg of the seven-hundred-mile race. The musher getting ready to begin was Kim's friend, Wendy. Jumping on the sled's runners, grabbing the handlebars, she yelled, "Hike!"

Kim cheered, jumping up and down in the creaky snow. "She's going to win it, I know. Women are winning these marathons lately!" Then, more quietly, she added, "I like 'Hike!' better. Don't you? 'Mush!' is so ordinary. I wonder what command I should use. I'll get my dogs as pups and we'll go through our endurance training together."

"*That*," Jason said, "would be perfect for you."

"Think so?" Kim looked immensely pleased.

"Sure. If your dogs can endure you, they can endure anything."

"Jason," Peter said quickly before Kim could respond, "did you finish interviewing that guy over there with the top-rated team?"

"Not yet." Jason pulled out his notebook and sauntered off, suddenly all business. There was nothing he liked more than gathering information.

He returned a few minutes later. "I got some good stuff. The drivers have to give the dogs regular rests, including some twelve-hour ones, and hot food. Even with all the care they get, some dogs don't make it."

Kim looked stunned.

"The best dog," Jason continued, "is in the lead harness followed by a sort of co-pilot. The rest are in pairs, with the strongest dogs closest to the sled."

Peter grinned at his brother. "Is that all you got?" he teased.

Kim took over. "Yeah, didn't you ask if they take turns stopping to wet on trees? Or do they do it all together?"

Peter watched, amazed, as Jason returned to the musher. They were so different from each other people barely believed they were brothers, much less twins. Peter was taller, skinnier and blonder than Jason, who much preferred reading to writing. That was fine with Peter. Without all the facts that Jason dug up, and without Kim's daring, Peter knew *The Green Street Reporter* wouldn't be worth his writing efforts.

"Where on earth is Milly?" someone behind Peter

asked. Finally, he thought. Now we're going to find out who it is people are worried about. Jason returned and listened too. "She's never missed the start before."

"Maybe she's sick," someone else offered. "Out there in the woods alone like she is, nobody'd know for months if she was sick."

"Or dead," another deeper voice said ominously.

"Naw, she's just out at checkpoint three. It's closest to her cabin. She's getting old, like her dog team. "We're bound to see her at checkpoint three."

"After what happened last year, maybe...well, she's turned into a real people-hater. But I'm sure she's all right."

"I don't know." It was the deep voice again. "She could've been dead for months already and nobody would know."

Peter felt a shiver climb his spine. This time it wasn't from the cold. "Did you hear that?" he whispered. "I *knew* something was wrong around here."

Kim nodded. "They must be talking about Milly Crenshaw. Wendy told me she's a real famous old frontierswoman. Someone's even writing a book about her. But lately...who knows? She might have gone loony or something."

Peter nodded. As usual, their story was taking an

unexpected turn. At checkpoint three they would have to get directions to her cabin, to find...what? A crazy old hermit, or maybe a frozen corpse. Either way the sled dog race would take days and might end up on the second page of *The Green Street Reporter* ...after the story of Milly Crenshaw.

2
The Trek Begins

"What do you mean we have to stick to our original story this time?" Peter asked his mother.

"I mean," she said, "that this race is interesting enough. It will be over in a few days. And it is the story we're being paid to cover."

"So, you've...I mean, we've *been* covering it." Peter kept his voice firm. "What will be so thrilling here at the third check point?"

"There are injuries, drop-outs, racers giving a hand to one another, all kinds of possible stories."

Peter sighed. They'd been cooped up in their stuffy old camper discussing this since breakfast. They seemed to be getting nowhere.

It was Jason who came up with the perfect argument. "You've never been out in the North Woods, have you?" he asked their parents. "Really out there, alone. Maybe you could write a better article if you went through more of what the racers do."

Peter and Kim both gave Jason grateful smiles.

Dad stood up, uncurling his lanky body as far as the camper's ceiling would allow. "We do have the snowshoes along, five pair. Why not venture out on them a little?" Dad gave Kim a wink; he must have known how desperate his daughter was to fling herself into the wilderness.

"I can give the kids the help they need," Dad continued. "It's pretty easy, actually."

Peter's hopes soared. One parent down, one to go. "I can't believe Milly Crenshaw doesn't interest you, Mom," he said. "She sounds like a super interview."

"She's been done." Mom stood up too, rubbing her fingers impatiently through her short dark hair.

"What do you mean, 'she's been done?' " Peter asked. "You mean there's nothing new we could possibly find out about her?"

Kim chimed in. "The people around here are all really surprised she hasn't shown up, especially at this checkpoint. She must be...well, sick, or caught in a trap or who knows what? Old people are always breaking hips, aren't they? What if she—?"

"I get your point, Kim." Mom turned to Dad. "Bob, for heaven's sake, be reasonable. Surely with all these worried people around here, somebody else will go investigate. Somebody who knows her and knows the way to her cabin."

Peter stared at his mother. Somebody else?

She clicked on the radio. At eight a.m. it was still well below zero, it said. High of fifteen above, some gusting winds. Snow was predicted but that was nothing unusual. No severe drop in temperature.

They all listened in the dim lamplight of their camper. Once the sun finally rises, Peter thought, maybe this detour won't worry Mom. Everything seems more dangerous in the dark.

Finally Peter gave it his best shot. "Mom, Milly may have been written about before, but never by *you*."

That did it. She smiled at last. "Okay. You win. But we have to plan and get ready *carefully*. You don't get many chances to make mistakes up here." She bent to kiss the top of Peter's head. "Not if you want to live to write your precious story."

Jason and Kim rushed to pack supplies, taking directions solemnly. They would need all their warm clothes, layer after layer. They would also need an ax, pocket knives, nylon twine, full canteens (eating snow was not a good way to quench thirst when it was this cold out), food, matches, the first aid kit, film for Dad, notebook and mini tape recorder for Mom.

Dad and Peter went out to get directions to Milly's cabin. The race official they asked frowned at them, paused, but then used a long stick he was holding to point due north of where they stood. "You can take that road there a ways, in your camper. Guess you'd better." He looked at them critically.

"Wait," Dad said, squinting in the direction the man pointed. "What road, where? You mean that space between trees? Is that a road?"

The man looked mildly offended, but he nodded and then proceeded to draw a map in the snow with his stick. Peter copied it down in the notebook he had handy. The directions seemed simple enough, but his hand, freed from its mitten long enough to write, was shaky, and not just from the cold.

How easy would it be to get lost out there? He could see the headline: *Family of five disappears. Search party gives up until spring thaw.* He shivered but smiled to himself.

"Thanks very much," Dad said to the official, and they returned to the camper.

"Some road," Mom muttered a few minutes later as they pulled away from checkpoint three and headed into the woods.

It took half an hour to reach the end of it, although it was only about ten miles long. Dad stopped the

camper, and everything, everyone was terribly quiet. Until Kim jumped out. "MILLY! HERE WE COME," she shouted to the dense mixture of pines, aspens and paper birches. And presumably to the snow. The snow was everywhere.

Peter realized that he had always thought of snow as simply a temporary blanket for everything else that existed. But here it was different, as if there *was* nothing else. There were trees and bare-branched shrubs and some jutting rocks, but mostly snow, far whiter and more perfect than in the city.

Strapping on the snowshoes was tricky, but Dad clearly knew what he was doing. "Now," he instructed them all, "just walk normally, not bowlegged. And don't let your legs tense up—you get cramps that way. Just let yourself go all loose and loppy."

They each followed Dad's lead around the camper.

"Don't try to lift them," he said. "The tails are supposed to drag some."

After Jason had taken his turn practicing, he examined his snowshoes' webbing. "Did you know—?"

Peter and Kim groaned.

"—that the first snowshoes were probably used in Siberia about 4,000 B.C.?" When he got no response he continued. "Maybe hunters were just copying the snowshoe hare."

"Kim rolled her eyes. "Did you know," she mocked Jason's voice, "that the first snowshoe hare was named Fred? His wife's name was Fluffy and they were direct ancestors of Thumper."

They all laughed, including Jason. Finally donning their backpacks, they set out into the woods. Peter checked his watch. It was almost 9:00. He tried to find the sun through the thick grey of the sky. This far north in January, the sun never ventured far from the horizon. But they would still have several hours of daylight.

The man had said Milly was only about an hour's trek from the end of the road. They would make it there and back easily if they didn't get lost. And if the gathering clouds meant nothing more than the flurries he had heard about on the radio.

3
Vanished

They had all studied the map so they could take turns leading and breaking the trail, alternating small hills and flat ice quite regularly. There seemed to be more water than land in the North Woods.

One lake didn't look so very large until they were crossing it...endlessly. Away from the trees' shelter, wind whipped at Peter's face and filled his eyes with tears. His eyelids kept trying to freeze shut.

"Make faces," Jason suggested from behind him. "It keeps the circulation going."

Then, just when Peter was sure he had suffered the worst, the lake began to mutter and groan under him.

"Mom! Dad!" the Green Street gang all started shouting at once. "The ice!"

Dad stopped and turned around, shaking his head and smiling. "It's perfectly safe," he said. "Those are just normal lake noises."

They continued walking. Peter unfastened and loosened some clothing now because he was sweating in spite of his cold face and numb fingers and toes. "Un-h-h," the lake said, and he shuddered. It was as if someone was under him trying to push through the ice.

"Don't worry," Dad said, and they plodded on.

At last they were free of that lake and, Peter knew, only a couple hundred yards from Milly's cabin. Everyone looked as exhausted as he felt, but since they were so close, there was no question of taking a rest. Besides, Dad told them to hurry. He was looking up at the sky. "The weather's going to turn sour on us."

"There it is!" Kim yelled after they had moved on for a few mintues. "I see it."

"It's so tiny," Mom said.

"No smoke coming out of the chimney," was Jason's ominous remark.

They slowed down as they neared the log cabin. Dead silence greeted them. Peter stared at the empty dog kennels and at the sled, half buried in snow.

"Look," Dad said and bounded ahead. "The door. It's wide open."

Peter felt tugged forward and back at the same time. He could see that snow had blown into the

cabin. It must be deserted. Or was poor Milly, what was left of her, waiting in there for someone to find her?

The cabin was empty. They could see that as soon as they entered, closing the door behind them. Mom and Dad stood by the door while the Green Street gang wandered slowly around the one small room that Milly called home.

At the center stood the bulky wood stove—still warm to the touch—which appeared to be both for heat and cooking. There was no actual kitchen, just a large wooden wash basin. The water in it was frozen, but only on the top. Peter poked his finger at it and the surface cracked sharply, making him jump.

A small handcrafted table stood against one wall with only one chair by it. Another chair lay on its side in the opposite corner of the room. The place was strangely empty, except for a lantern perched crookedly on a window ledge, a frying pan containing meat and congealed grease on the stove, and a plate and fork on a nearby chopping block.

"What's happened here?" Peter asked.

"From the look of things," Mom said gently, "she's wandered off or something."

"Then we'll go find her," Kim said. She rushed back outside to strap on her snowshoes.

Mom shook her head. "We should go back for

help, for a search party or something."

"I don't know." Dad's gaze turned to the sky again. "Snow's on its way. Could be a lot."

It occurred to Peter that if they went back now, their parents probably wouldn't let them return again with the search party. He wanted to be in the middle of whatever action there was going to be.

He hit on an idea. "Maybe," he said to their parents, "you'd better go back without us."

"And leave you here alone?" Mom stared at him.

Luckily, Jason followed Peter's lead. "Milly might come back any minute," he said. "Cold and weak. We should build a fire and keep it going for her. The smoke might even help her find her way back."

"The boys have a point, Martha," Dad said. "And it looks like it'll be safer here than out there. The kids won't get caught in any storm. They can be here to help Milly if she returns and..." Dad paused for a moment. "We can make better time on our own."

"I guess," Mom said uncertainly, "that time is beginning to look like a problem. But why don't you go alone then? I'll stay here."

"It's never a good idea to be out in the wilderness alone," Dad answered.

"The way Milly must be," Jason added.

Before Mom could think of any more objections, Peter went outside to grab some logs and kindling.

Jason joined him.

"What's going on?" Kim asked impatiently. She was still waiting, apparently, to lead the Grant-Riley search party.

Jason stayed behind to explain the plan to her while Peter carried in his load of wood. Dad built a fire in the stove, and Mom removed some of the supplies from her backpack, doubt etched on her face.

When Jason and Kim came back in, Kim was still stubbornly snowshoed, a fact everybody ignored. Her glasses fogged up in the warming cabin, and she left them that way.

"Be sure to keep this fire going strong," Mom said. "And stay inside." She glanced anxiously back and forth between Peter and Jason. *Can I trust you?* her expression seemed to ask.

"We should be back in…" Dad chewed on his lip, figuring. "Depending on the weather and on how fast we can get the sheriff…three to four hours, I'd say."

Mom kissed each of the kids and hugged them tight. "I don't know…"

"Stop worrying, Mom," Jason said. "We'll be fine. What could happen?"

Peter hurried to add, "We'll just curl up here by the fire." He, for one, had no intention of braving those woods again on their own. All he wanted to do

24

was to wait for the official search party. And if he had to, he would tie Kim to a chair.

"We have to take most of the supplies," Dad said as he gave his goodbye hugs. "But we left you the food. Eat up. You must be starved."

Their parents left, and Peter and Jason pulled off some of their outer garments. Kim did not, Peter noticed, but she would get overheated soon enough.

Jason moved one of Milly's chairs over to the stove, sat and lifted his feet to wiggle them in the heat. Peter joined him and they both leaned back to close their eyes. It felt so good to sit, to be free of mittens and hats, to be warm and relaxed.

"Maybe we'll get snowed in here for the night," Peter murmured. His mouth didn't want to move more than absolutely necessary. "That would be...nice."

But Peter's drifting off was abruptly halted when Kim shouted, "What is the MATTER with you two jerks? There's an old lady out there, maybe freezing to death, and all you can do is sit there!"

Peter's eyes, startled open, followed Kim as she paced awkwardly, feverishly, in her snowshoes. Still, his body felt as heavy as Milly's old stove.

"Okay," Kim continued. "Sit all you want. I'll go by myself. And if I die out there, you'll be my murderers...and Milly's." She clumped out

the door.

Jason gave an exasperated sigh, but he got up with Peter to catch her. Maybe, Peter thought, they *would* have to tie her up to keep her in the cabin.

But outside, she was nowhere in sight. Jason pointed at her tracks leading to the back.

Then they heard her voice. "COME HERE!" she was shouting. "QUICK!"

They found her pointing at something in the snow. It was a single set of human tracks blurred by a long imprint and leading into the woods. Clearly something had been dragged away. And that something, or someone, had left a stain in the snow. The stain was the vivid red of fresh blood.

4
Forced To Disobey

"Now," Peter said when they had returned to the cabin and the fire, "we'd better make some plans. Carefully, remember?" He directed this mostly to Kim. "We don't just run out and follow this trail."

"We don't?" Kim asked defiantly.

"No. We can make our plans while we eat."

They each pulled out a bag of gorp and stuffed their mouths with the mixture of granola, nuts, sunflower seeds, raisins, and chocolate chips. Jason finished off the water in his canteen and then looked around the cabin. "That's odd."

"What?" Peter asked.

"No bucket."

Peter and Kim looked around too.

"Milly must have a bucket to melt snow in, or to get water under the lake ice. It's not that she didn't have anything." Jason continued. "It's that everything's gone. Look at all those empty pegs and racks all over the walls. She probably had traps and weapons and skins and all kinds of things hanging on those. All stolen."

"Who'd steal an old bucket?" Kim asked.

"Someone who needed one badly enough," Peter said. "It's useful, not valuable."

"Maybe." Jason borrowed Peter's canteen, took a few sips and then frowned at him. "This is practically full. Don't be dumb, Pete. You've got to drink. You can get dehydrated in the cold just like in the heat."

"Yeah, yeah," Peter snatched back his canteen but did take several long drinks.

"I thought we were going to plan," Kim said with her mouth full.

"Well, we've got to follow that trail, of course," Peter said. "It should be fresh enough. It looks like this all just happened, earlier this morning. The stove was warm. The water was just beginning to freeze. No animal has gotten to the meat. Milly may have been sitting right where I am now, not more than an hour or so ago."

"Do you think there's a body at the end of that trail?" Kim asked in a hushed voice.

"Well, there must be something," Jason answered. "And I'd sure like to find out what."

Kim nodded and then said, as though she just happened to remember, "Well, I did find some clues."

Peter and Jason looked at her, startled.

Triumphantly she pulled something out of her jacket pocket. In the dim light it looked to Peter like a scrap of brown paper. "Blood-matted fur," Kim announced. "Coarse, like a weasel's, or a beaver's."

Jason shook his head. "Milly was probably wearing a fur jacket. So what?"

Kim dug into her pocket once more. "Was she wearing the animal's foot too?" Between her fingers was what appeared to be a claw.

"Where'd you find those things?" Jason asked.

"Right in the imprint the body made."

Peter thought for a moment. Jason mumbled that weasels are white, not brown, in winter. Kim tapped her foot impatiently.

Finally Peter said, "We don't know how this woman dressed. She could've made jewelry out of claws or teeth, right? Besides, whatever was dragged out there was sure bigger than a weasel. Probably bigger than a beaver, too."

Kim shrugged and stuck the fur and claw back into her pocket. "They're clues, though. And if we sit here much longer, we won't find any more."

Quickly they packed up the supplies left by their

parents, bundled up again and left the cabin shut tight against the mounting wind. The snow that was beginning to fall made Peter uneasy, but he said nothing.

"We've got to hurry," Kim said as they all strapped on their snowshoes. "This snow's going to ruin our case. It'll cover everything up."

Peter pushed away thoughts of warm cabins and embraced, instead, the pursuit of their "case," as Kim had put it. It really was theirs now. Yes, they were disobeying their parents and yes, they would be in trouble later. But nobody else would be able to find much of anything after a few hours of this snow.

In fact, Milly's disappearance could remain a mystery forever without the efforts of the Green Street gang.

5
The Trail Goes Cold

The blood-stained trail made a loop at first, and then ended up parallel to the path their family had taken to the cabin. The snow here was not deep or soft enough to require snowshoes, they soon discovered. They should have known that since the feet they were following managed just fine. These feet knew exactly where they were going, Peter thought to himself... and the best way to get there.

The Green Street gang attached their snowshoes to their backpacks and continued, still within sight of their earlier path. Peter realized that, if they had come earlier, they might have seen everything. A few yards away, through some skinny birches, would have been someone dragging something. But who and what?

The trail veered sharply away from their own as

soon as they reached the lake. Thank goodness, they would be staying in the trees and not crossing that dreaded lake again. Even so, Peter's head began to ache from the battering of the wind. The snowflakes, so delicate and pretty by themselves at rest, turned into a sandpapery mass in the cold wind.

"I read somewhere," Jason said when Peter had complained about all the snow, "that it might be a myth that there are no two snowflakes alike. There are so many, uniqueness may be impossible."

"Um-m-m." Peter didn't care if they were *all* identical. They were making his life miserable.

After about thirty minutes, Jason, who was in the lead at the time, stopped abruptly, his head down. Through the blowing snow, Peter couldn't quite see what his brother was looking at, so he caught up with him and stared down into the jagged, rocky mouth of a ravine. The sun, even at almost noon, was low at their backs and the ravine was in purplish shadow. It could have been very deep, but Peter couldn't tell.

The trail ended here. Whatever had been dragged must have been lifted and thrown. But not without considerable trouble, from the looks of the snow. Peter was astonished to find no footprints leading away from the ravine.

"Do you think she's down there?" Kim asked quietly, as if at a grave.

"I don't know," Jason said.

Now what? The question hung in the air. Peter knew he would be expected to answer first. The wind was kicking at him, coaxing him. If this wasn't a blizzard starting up, it surely was a pretty good imitation.

"We'd better head back," Peter said, "or our tracks will be blown away, and we could end up lost."

Jason picked up a chunk of snow and tossed it into the side of a tree. Pieces of it scattered between them. He trudged away and reached for another one but instead of throwing it, he stopped. "What's this?"

About fifteen feet to the left of the dead-ended trail was a single footprint, deep into a drift.

"How can there be only one?" Peter asked, heat returning to his insides.

"The rest have been covered up," Jason pointed out. "Somebody didn't notice how deep this one was. They backed away from here, sweeping the snow, probably with a branch."

"They couldn't have done it forever," Kim said. "Let's go look behind that stand of pine trees over there. That looks like the best direction to me."

Wait, Peter was thinking. We've got to get back. But he didn't say it. They probably wouldn't listen to him anyway. He looked back at the bootprints they had just made. They were very visible, but for how much longer?

"Here!" Kim hollered from behind the pines.

Peter rushed to join Jason and Kim. There, at the edge of a huge clearing, was a single set of human tracks, snowshoed this time.

They followed their quarry's example and plunged after it in their own showshoes, Kim first, then Jason and Peter. Sure enough, the snow seemed to be incredibly deep here. How far might they have sunk in their boots? Peter wondered.

After several minutes, Peter heard a strange noise come out of Kim. Straight ahead of them, about fifty yards away, was a sight that made Peter's heart stop cold. It was a gigantic creature, brown and husky and long-legged. It swung its massive, antlered head to stare at them.

They waited, and so did the bull moose.

"How dangerous could he be?" Jason asked. "He's just a big deer, you know. The biggest."

"And meanest," Peter said. "Some of the drivers..." He gulped a few times and continued hoarsely. "They said that coming across a moose was the most dangerous thing that could happen to them during the race. Lots of dogs and drivers have been stomped on. Killed, some of them."

Trying to remember exactly what the drivers had said they did when coming upon a moose, Peter

36

slowly moved to the side of the trail. One step, two, three. "Okay, listen," he whispered. "If we want to go on...*if* we really want to, we don't confront this moose, okay?" He beckoned in slow motion for them to follow him. "We have to circle way around."

"We'll lose the trail," Kim protested, but she too was whispering.

"Maybe we should just turn back," Jason suggested.

Peter gave him a surprised look.

"Just sit and think for a minute," Kim added. "Regroup. Let the moose go on his way."

Apparently, common sense could be introduced to them by a huge, hairy creature. Peter smiled and turned toward the trees from which they had emerged several minutes earlier.

They backtracked with some difficulty against the wind. Some of the gusts stopped them dead in their tracks for a while. When Peter blinked his eyes clear of snow and tears, he stared ahead. Fear gnawed inside his belly. Jason and Kim must have been similarly struck by the vast expanse of white ahead of them. Smooth, undisturbed snow. Their snowshoe prints had been blown away, completely.

"Don't panic," Peter said more to himself than to the others. "Just try not to turn at all. Straight on should be where we came out of those trees. Maybe our tracks inside the woods are more protected."

"Yeah. We'll find them," Kim added.

They trudged ahead. Peter's legs ached; he couldn't loosen the muscles enough. If he were any more tense, he was sure he would snap somewhere inside. The moose had unnerved them all, and now this.

His worst fear was realized when they finally reached the woods only to find more smooth snow. It was as if human beings had never been anywhere near the place...or shouldn't have been.

They were looking less and less like themselves and more like elaborate snowmen. Flakes settled even in their eyelashes in spite of the wind.

"I feel like we're at the North Pole," Kim said rubbing snow from her glasses with her mitten.

"Actually," Jason said, "this is nothing like the North Pole. It only snows about an inch in a whole year at the Poles."

Kim and Peter glared at him.

"Of course," he added quickly, "the snow that falls there stays forever and this stuff will melt... eventually."

"That's comforting, Jason," Peter said.

They found some dense trees where wind was less of a problem, and they curled up into tight balls. But Peter knew that this would not be enough shelter for long. This storm could go on for hours. Nobody in the whole world knew where they were. They had matches, but Peter doubted they could light a fire in the icy swirls of wind encircling them. They were doomed.

Even so, the thought flashed in his mind: What a great story this would make for The Reporter.

Maybe, he thought then, someone else will have to write it.

6
Snow Shelter

"According to how recent the winter solstice was," Jason's voice was infuriatingly calm and scientific, "we've got about two hours." He paused. "Then it will be dark."

It was time for action, no doubt about that. Peter sprang up and then groaned. His body felt as if it had frozen into a ball.

"Okay," he said with more confidence than he felt, "we need to build a shelter. Ideas anyone?"

Jason stood up more slowly. "Mom and Dad took the ax but maybe we could find enough broken branches."

"And tie them together with what?" Kim asked. "I say we use what we've got the most of. Snow."

"Yeah," Peter agreed. "Why didn't I think of that? Just like the snow forts we build at home. Remember how warm it always is inside packed snow?"

New life had been injected into them all. The Green Street gang had a plan, and it was a good one.

They decided to build their shelter at the edge of the clearing because there was so much snow there. But they argued for a while about which direction the opening should face. Peter wanted it toward the west to catch the sunlight as long as possible, but Jason figured it should face east, to catch the first rays of the sun the next morning. Because of the westerly wind, they settled on Jason's plan. Peter hated thinking about morning, but maybe they had to.

"Who wants to jump in to see how firm the snow is?" Peter asked. "And how deep." He pictured one of them being swallowed by an ocean of snow.

Kim held out her arms and jumped into the snow. The boys joined her, jumping around and around, sometimes to their knees or above. Now they could be confident of the snow's firmness, but they still weren't sure of its depth.

"We'd better build up a mound first," Peter said, "in case the ground's closer than we think."

Thankfully, the wind had lost some of its cruelty by this time, but the temperature was dropping fast. The snow continued to fall.

Without shovels or even scoops, their snow mound was slow in growing. Heap it up, pat it down,

42

heap it up. By the time it satisfied them, they were all sweating and panting. "At least we're not cold any more," Kim said.

The tunneling was more fun. They took turns digging and scooping out snow. Then when it was hard to reach, they stuck their feet in to kick and scrape away at the inside.

Once, while resting, Kim looked over her shoulder to the clearing. "I just remembered that moose out there."

"He's long gone," Peter reassured her.

"And bears are all hibernating," she added. "But what about wolves?"

Only...dangerous...if...attacked," Jason, who was tunneling, said between breaths.

They worked in silence for another half hour. With the mound, the snow did end up being deep enough for a three-person shelter, but it would be a tight squeeze. Good, Peter told himself. Their combined body heat would raise the temperature inside.

While one dug, the other two snacked, drank, and rested. They each kept one pair of mittens dry and dug with another pair. The sun continued to sink, gold turning to shadowy bronze.

Finally the shelter was declared finished. "Think it'll hold?" Peter asked.

"Even if it doesn't cave in," Kim said. "I don't

know…a whole night in there…"

They looked at each other somberly. The silence was broken only by their ragged breathing, and then by a sharp, distant sound.

"What was that?" Peter whispered. "A wolf?"

"Not a chance," Kim said. "You were with us at the wolf exhibit at the Science Museum. Wolves sound more like this; 'Ahhooohh…Yip! Yip! Yip!'"

Peter and Jason both shushed her.

Ahhooohh… Yip! Yip! Yip! It was a distant answer to Kim's howl.

Jason and Peter automatically closed the distance between them."Nice going, Kim," Jason said. "I think you've got one in love with you."

Kim poked Jason but stopped the animal sounds.

"Time to go inside, I guess," Peter said, inching toward their small entry way.

"First we have to make a hole in the top, for air." Jason grabbed a branch. Carefully he drilled it through the roof. It went through easily. A little too easily, Peter thought, but the roof held when the branch was withdrawn.

"Ladies first," Jason said.

"Gladly." Kim slid through the opening and dropped down. "Hand me some balsam or spruce branches to cushion the floor."

When they had all settled in, Peter felt mournful.

He realized that his parents would have gotten back to Milly's cabin long ago. They would be frantic. He wished the three of them had stayed put.

"What's that?" Jason asked. "It's that sound again. Not Kim's wolf, the other one."

"It's closer," Jason said. "It could even be right outside, the way these walls smother sound."

It was darker in the shelter than outside. They all stared, unblinking, up at the opening. It had been a greyish oval but now most of it was gone, blackened by something leaning in to sniff at them. A deep-throated growl filled Peter with a terror he could practically taste.

They weren't going to freeze to death after all. Instead, they were about to become somebody's dinner.

7
Visitors

The entryway was clear again. But then came the laughter. A human voice. "Great ghosts! Is it man, beast, or spirit in there?"

"We're saved!" Kim yelled and elbowed her way out of the shelter. Jason followed and then Peter. There before them was what appeared to be a human. At least the leathery face was. The rest of the head and the body was draped with furs and skins.

"Percy here says you're all right," the creature said, gesturing toward a husky who sat off to one side, head cocked. "So you must be. Puny though. What are you? Children of some kind?"

"You're Milly Crenshaw, aren't you?" Kim's voice was unusually hushed.

"Milly who?"

The Green Street gang looked at each other. It had

48

to be Milly, didn't it? Who else?

The woman gazed at them, and her frown deepened. Her skin looked like dried mud. "Oh, rat raisins! You'd better come with me. Otherwise you'd leave me an awful mess come spring. Human flesh don't exactly freeze and thaw pretty."

They obeyed, of course. What else could they do? But Peter remembered the unpretty sight that he had expected to see when finally finding her. If she was alive and well, whose bloody body had been dragged to the ravine? Maybe this woman was the murderer.

It was a short, easy trek to the woman's shelter. She must have doubled back after crossing the clearing to throw off trackers. Her shelter was an impressive lean-to built between two trees. The slanted roof was covered with enough nesting material for a thousand squirrels. Insulation. Peter figured this structure had taken hours, even days to build, so she had been planning on staying here all along.

In front of the lean-to's open side, a safe six feet away, was a big fire pit they gratefully huddled around. Peter felt blood rush to his fingers as he held them to the fire. They began to sting and itch, but he didn't pull his hands back. He would regain his strength. He would have to. They might have to defend themselves.

The woman was silent now, stirring something in

a pot that hung low over the fire. Hot food. His stomach screamed for joy. But what concoction would she have created out of wild animals?

This woman was much smaller than he had expected. Her eyes appeared to be black, the chopped off bangs poking out from her hood were dry and white.

"You are Milly Crenshaw," Peter managed to say at last. The smell steaming over to them from the pot had moistened his mouth. "A lot of people are worried about you."

She laughed deep from her chest. "So worried they sent out three babies to hunt me down, eh?"

"We weren't exactly sent," Peter confessed. "We just couldn't stay away."

"Figures." She was fiddling nimbly with sheets of birch bark and some small, straight twigs. Then she stopped suddenly. "Rat raisins! I suppose there's folks out hunting after *you* now."

"They wouldn't know where to look," Jason said.

"Are you hiding?" Kim asked. "Did you do something...uh...wrong?"

"Wrong? Yes, I daresay. I'm still alive. That's wrong enough, eh? Now come fill your bellies." She offered each of them a bowl-shaped piece of birch bark and a set of twig-chopsticks. "Sorry about these utensils. Wasn't expectin' company."

She dished out something that appeared to be stew, although none of the ingredients tasted quite like anything Peter had eaten before.

"Could do more for you if it weren't winter," Milly said. "This woods is full of food if you know where to look, and when."

Peter was now warming from the inside as well as outside. He was getting drowsy and didn't dare wait any longer to speak of practical matters. "Can you guide us back to your cabin?"

Milly was gathering wood and examining it closely. "Now, we have to build up this fire for the night."

"But," Peter tried again. "Aren't we—?"

"Start with plenty of regular firewood— hardwood's best. Then add some wet wood, hear?" She busied herself with the wood, deflecting any further questions. "Finally comes the layer of *green* wood that'll burn slowly for hours and leave us some nice coals come morning. Got that now?"

Without waiting for an answer or any more questions, Milly disappeared into a shadowed corner of her lean-to and then emerged brushing her teeth with a fuzzy stick.

"Ms. Crenshaw, we have to get back."

"Tonight? Are you crazy? This storm's nothing to mess with. Curl up in here when you're ready to stop yammering and go to sleep."

"But..." Peter swallowed. "But the storm's over and our parents will be—"

"Glad you've taken shelter. Now be still. That's a good boy." She returned to her corner and Peter stared up at the night sky.

The storm *was* over. He was sure of it, just as he was sure that Milly knew these woods well enough to guide them by her lantern light. What was going on?

"I suppose," Jason said quietly, "Mom and Dad will figure that we've found shelter."

"Maybe they've had to do the same thing," Kim said. "Maybe they never made it back with the sheriff at all. That way, they'd think we were still safe at the cabin all this time."

"They got more than they bargained for on *this* assignment," Peter said. "But they'll see how much better their story will be because of all this."

"I KNEW IT!" Milly burst out of the shelter and stopped just short of leaping into the flames. Peter's heart jumped into his throat. "Reporters! Another fool story...'Milly Crenshaw, North Country Loon,' or some such nonsense. I'm sick of it. Every year at race time, it's the same blasted mess of nosy reporters sniffing at me.

"Last year was the limit. A television crew. A

bookwriter pushing contracts under my nose, asking me questions too personal to ask your own mother. Well, this year I could've fooled 'em. This year it would've been 'Milly Crenshaw, Dead at Last.' Except you brats had to get yourselves near-killed, and I didn't have the good sense to leave you to it. Reporters' brats—just my luck."

Peter glanced at Kim and Jason who were listening to Milly's tirade with their mouths hanging open. He hoped they would resist the urge to brag that they were more than "reporters' brats," that they were reporters themselves. Milly looked mad enough to kill anyone with a pencil in his hand and a question in his eyes.

He remembered the way his mother had said, about Milly, "She's been done." She sure had been.

"I'm sorry, Ma'am," Peter said. "But we just came for the race." That, he told himself, was no lie.

"And you just stumbled across my cabin, I suppose, on a stroll from the checkpoint. It's only just shy of twenty miles out of the way."

"Did you take everything out of your cabin?" Jason asked, pulling Milly's fiery gaze away from Peter. "Did you leave that trail?"

Suddenly Milly was laughing again, so hard she had to bend and support herself on her knees. "That was some trick, eh? Took a mighty big beaver to look like the dragged body of poor ol' Milly. Terrible waste, though. Would've like to save the pelt."

Peter remembered the ravine and thought of a dead beaver lying there. At least it wasn't a human body!

"Sheriff Olson, now, he's always been a good boy," Milly continued, more seriously. "He's got a badge now, so he'll thrash around for a time, looking for me. But this storm helped me out. What clues could it leave? Not a one. They'll give up on looking for an old lady before long. Then I can go back to my home. By the time somebody sees me again, maybe the reporters will have gone on to pester some other poor soul."

With that, she retreated back into her lean-to. The Green Street gang followed, accepting the musty-smelling blankets she tossed their way.

Milly's dog, probably the only one left of her old team, sighed before curling into a ball near the fire.

It was easy to feel a little sorry for Milly, but not for long. Because Peter couldn't help but notice that she was now talking as though her plan hadn't been spoiled at all, as though she had no intention of bringing them back to explain everything.

What if...? Peter stiffened. What if she was planning to leave them in the shelter during the night? Sneak off, continue her flight from reporters and the sheriff? She might just count on the "babies" to stay hopelessly lost and eventually...

Kim and Jason looked about to drop into a deep sleep. Kim still appeared to be quietly in awe of Milly, and Jason... well, he was probably suspicious too. It was his nature. But he looked utterly exhausted. Peter couldn't discuss this with them now, even if he wanted to. Milly was within earshot. It would have to be up to him to stay awake, or at least alert enough to catch Milly if she decided to desert them.

8
No Words

The first sunlight poked hot fingers at Peter's eyelids and whispers floated around his head. The thunk of logs being tossed into a hissing fire brought him fully awake. He saw a figure by the fire. It was Kim, but Milly wasn't there. Even Percy was gone.

"Kim! Where's Milly?"

"She went into the woods for a ... visit," Kim said.

"Thank goodness!"

"Why? What's the matter with you?"

Peter closed his eyes and shook his head. He couldn't possibly tell Kim now what he had feared the night before. It would sound crazy.

"We've been talking, Peter." Kim whispered since Jason was still asleep. "Milly and I. About why she's here, who she is and who she used to be."

"And?"

Kim shook her head and sighed. "I don't know. Milly asked me—can you believe this?—*which story* do I want? And then she told me things that didn't fit together. Like, she said she became a drifter during the Great Depression and never married. But then she told me her husband and children had been brutally murdered. She blamed 'civilization.' The next minute she said she'd led a perfectly ordinary life until the government decided she was a Communist during the fifties and...well, I just want the truth."

The fire crackled and Peter felt the heat seep in. "Kim, leave her alone."

"What? Why?"

He wanted to say that they *needed* Milly to be nice to them, not in another rage. But that didn't feel like the full answer. So he shrugged.

"I just want to know her," Kim whispered.

"Maybe she doesn't *want* to be known."

Jason crept over to them. "What's going on?"

"Breakfast!" Milly screeched at them, returning from the woods. Peter nearly jumped out of his parka.

Nobody spoke while they ate. A duet of friendly *chick-a-dee-dee-dee's* greeted them from overhead, and then the birds tipped their black caps to them.

"Did you know," Jason said after clearing his

throat, "that some bird species *shiver* most of the winter, to keep their body temperature up."

They looked to Milly who nodded but said nothing.

Jason shrugged. "Do you think they'll be sending helicopters out to look for us?" he asked.

Peter felt himself blush. Why hadn't he thought of that last night instead of panicking the way he had about Milly? They didn't really need her that much. That big clearing was nearby. They could build a fire.

"Might take hours to get one," Milly said. "I'll take you back. Don't worry."

They sat and drank a watery tea in silence.

"Well," Kim said grumpily, "let's go then."

Milly got up to douse the fire, but it seemed to Peter that, otherwise, she was leaving her shelter as it was, filled with her belongings. She must have been planning to return. Maybe, he thought, she could.

He noticed Jason was examining Milly's things now, taking mental notes. If Peter wanted to know, later, what kinds of traps Milly used and what kinds of weapons (no guns in sight), Jason would be able to fill him in. He even stopped to read the titles of three battered books stacked by Milly's bedding. What would a woman like Milly read, over and

over?

The trek back was surprisingly easy. No blizzard, no worry about tracks or taking a wrong turn somewhere.

Several minutes after they had left the lean-to, Milly stopped so abruptly, the Green Street gang ran right into her. "Are we—?" Peter started to ask, but Milly shushed him harshly. She pointed her mitten straight ahead. There, directly in their path, stood a doe. She looked ready to flee but aimed her curious eyes at them first, ears and tail twitching.

Peter held his breath. All around them he noticed for the first time a light shower of glittering snow crystals. It was falling magically from a bright, unclouded sky.

Jason, from behind him, whispered, "Peter, you've got to write about this. It's something...special."

Peter merely shook his head. How could this sight...this feeling be put into words?

Milly seemed to agree, because she said firmly, "Some things can't be written." The deer stepped delicately from their path, on her way.

And they continued on theirs. Peter was directly behind Milly, and he noticed that she did not disturb the deer's heart-shaped tracks. He stepped over them too. It occurred to him that some people, faced with that deer in that setting, wouldn't hesitate to approach it, to try to touch it, or maybe even to shoot it for sport. But he felt good about what they had done...nothing.

Later, Milly stopped again and turned. "This is as far as I go. Due west, through the middle of those trees up ahead, you'll find the cabin." She strode past them and, as unexpectedly as she had appeared the night before, she was gone.

They didn't make it all the way to the door before it swung open and Mom and Dad rushed to embrace them. Everyone was crying and laughing at the same time.

Inside at last, Peter was not surprised to find a young man in a uniform, apparently Sheriff Olson. He had an odd smile on his face.

"You kids are darn lucky," the sheriff said. "Found shelter and food on your own, did you?"

Peter did not even hesitate before nodding.

"Boy Scout training," Jason explained.

"Pure animal instincts," Kim added.

Sheriff Olson's smile broadened. "No sign of a crafty old lady out there, eh? About as tall as your mom here and mean as a wolverine? No? You're sure?"

Meanwhile, Mom's and Dad's joy and relief were giving way rapidly to fury. Throughout the scolding, the sheriff watched them all, shaking his head, and then slowly pulled on his parka. "Well, you folks know the way back. I've got things to attend to, like calling back my search party. There's nothing more for me to do here. Bye now."

In the silent tension that followed his departure, Mom said, "So, she's out there hiding, I guess. But from whom?"

"From us," Peter said. He watched out the window as the sheriff's snowmobile disappeared. Milly had said the sheriff was a "good boy." He wasn't about to betray her, but what would they tell everybody back at the race?

There's nothing to tell, Peter answered himself. He felt only a twinge of regret about the story that might have been. Mostly, he felt deep satisfaction.

"We'd better head out to the finish line," he told the others. His gaze was still set on the woods that had, for one whole day, been their home. "Those drivers are going to be brimming over with stories. And we're the ones to write them down."

Green Street Mystery

Don't miss the other
exciting adventures of
The Green Street Gang
starring
Peter, Kim and Jason
as they travel around the world
uncovering and solving
new mysteries

CRESTWOOD HOUSE

Mankato, MN, U.S.A.